The Slime Wars

**Want more books by Debbie Dadey?
Then check out . . .**

Swamp Monster in Third Grade

And don't forget . . .

by Debbie Dadey and Marcia Thornton Jones

The Slime Wars

by Debbie Dadey
with her son, Nathan Dadey

Illustrated by
Bill Basso

A
LITTLE APPLE
PAPERBACK

SCHOLASTIC INC.

NEW YORK   TORONTO   LONDON   AUCKLAND   SYDNEY
MEXICO CITY   NEW DELHI   HONG KONG BUENOS AIRES

To Nathan Dadey, a wonderful son — DD
To Debbie Dadey — ND

No part of this publication may be reproduced in whole or in part, stored in a retrieval system, or transmitted in any form or by any means, electronic, mechanical, photocopying, recording, or otherwise, without written permission of the publisher. For information regarding permission, write to Scholastic Inc., Attention: Permissions Department, 557 Broadway, New York, NY 10012.

ISBN 0-439-42442-9

Text copyright © 2003 by Debra S. Dadey and Nathan Dadey
Illustrations copyright © 2003 by Scholastic Inc.
SCHOLASTIC, LITTLE APPLE, and associated logos are trademarks and/or registered trademarks of Scholastic Inc.

12 11 10 9 8 7 6 5 4 3 2 1   3 4 5 6 7 8/0

Printed in the U.S.A.
First printing, February 2003

40

CONTENTS

Chapter 1
THE LINE

There's a line down the middle of our street. Some people think it's for car lanes, but I know better. It's the dividing line. Patrick, Will, and I live on the south side of Daleside Drive, the boy's side. We live a few houses away from one another. The girls live side by side on the north side. Tammy and Karen are sisters and Angela is their next-door neighbor. Anyone who steps over the line is declaring war.

That's what happened this summer — the terrible trio declared war. Patrick, Will, and I were minding our own business playing basketball in my driveway when it all started.

"Guard him, Justin," Patrick yelled at me. Guarding Will is not an easy task. Will is at least three inches taller than me, and probably ten pounds heavier. Since Will has the advantage, Justin and I usually play two against one. I tried to block Will's shot, but the ball sailed high over my head, and he made the basket anyway.

I retrieved the ball and passed it to Patrick, who jumped up in the air and made a spectacular basket. The basketball went through the hoop just as someone yelled, "Bombs away!" Tammy, Karen, and Angela zoomed by on their bikes and launched their torpedoes. The torpedoes were old tennis balls. That wouldn't have been so bad, except that the tennis balls had holes in them with rotten eggs inside.

"Duck," Will shouted, but it was too late. I had egg yolk all over my Chicago Bulls T-shirt and Patrick had egg slime on his face. He looked like an omelet. Will was the only one who hadn't been egged. But that didn't keep him from getting mad.

"I'm going to get those girls!" he yelled.

"By the time I'm done with them, they'll feel like scrambled eggs."

"Those girls are nothing but big chickens," Patrick complained. "They didn't even stop."

"Why would they want to declare war anyway?" I asked. "We haven't done anything mean to them in a long time." I couldn't remember exactly when it had become the girls against the boys on our street. It must have started around second grade, when it had been fun to tease the girls and play little pranks. Now, it was practically a tradition. Frankly, I was tired of the whole thing.

Patrick looked a little embarrassed. "Well," he said slowly, "it might have something to do with the other day."

"What did you do?" I asked, figuring Patrick could have done anything and probably had.

"It was sort of an accident," Patrick explained, wiping egg off his freckled cheek with the bottom of his *Star Wars* T-shirt, "but the girls probably didn't think so."

"Let's hear it," Will told him. "What happened?"

Patrick shrugged. "I was eating at Burger World with Ralph. We were just fooling around." Ralph is Patrick's sixteen-year-old brother. Most of the time Ralph acts like he's eleven, like us.

"I stepped on a ketchup package and it squirted Tammy right in the face," Patrick said. "She looked like a squished tomato."

Will laughed and bounced the basketball on the driveway. "That must have been a big improvement."

"This isn't funny," I told my friends. "Patrick started the war again, and now the girls are going to make our lives miserable." I remembered the last war. It had been last year and it hadn't been pretty. Between the toilet paper and peanut butter on my bicycle and the Vaseline inside my in-line skates, life had been pretty rotten. I wanted to avoid another battle like that.

"We can't let them get away with egging us," Will reminded me.

"It'll wash off," I said. "If we leave them alone, they'll leave us alone. We'll be even. And the war will be over."

"That's not any fun," Patrick said. Patrick was the kind of kid who never let a chance for trouble go by. "I have an idea that will make the girls sorry they even looked at your house. By the time we get finished with them, they'll wish tennis balls had never been invented."

"What are you talking about?" Will asked him.

I didn't want to listen so I walked over to my mailbox. I grabbed a big stack of mail. I'd been waiting for a special letter. All I wanted to do was go inside with the mail, see if my letter had come, and wash the egg off my shirt. The slime was soaking through and sticking to my body.

But Patrick followed me to my mailbox and grinned. "Do you still have that feather pillow upstairs on your bed?"

I nodded my head slowly. Whatever

Patrick had planned with my feather pillow couldn't be good. Patrick patted me on the shoulder, and I had the feeling that the war was in full swing whether I liked it or not.

Chapter 2
THE MALL

I rifled through the mail. "Darn," I said. "It still hasn't come."

Will shook his head. "Just forget about *The Slime Wars*. They're never going to ask you to be on that stupid game show."

"You don't know that," I told him. "It could happen. We could all win new bikes and a ton of money."

"Yeah, right," Patrick said. "And my brother is really from Mars. Forget about that slimy show. Let's concentrate on getting back at the girls. Grab your feather pillow and meet us at the main mall entrance in a half hour. I have the perfect plan."

Patrick and Will didn't give me time to argue. They took off on their bikes toward

Will's house. Patrick shouted over his shoulder, "Bring the pillow in your backpack."

I shrugged and went into my house to take a quick shower. The egg was already starting to harden. It felt like quick-drying cement. Of course, it wouldn't have surprised me if the girls *had* thrown in a little cement with the eggs. After a shower, I stretched out on my bed. My head rested on my feather pillow. What did Patrick want with it?

I grabbed the pillow and stuffed it in my backpack. It barely fit. I felt like a hunchback with the bulging pack on my back and probably looked like one, too. A hunchback riding his old BMX bike down the street.

Patrick's and Will's bikes were already locked up in the bike rack when I got to the mall. I stashed mine next to theirs. Patrick and Will were waiting at our usual meeting place, right inside the main entrance, in front of Arcade Castle. Will had a strip of tickets he'd won and was cashing them in for a mini water gun.

Patrick still had egg on his freckled face. "Did you bring the pillow?" he asked.

I nodded. "What do you have in mind?" I asked. "I don't want to do anything mean."

Patrick laughed. "Oh, no. We're going to do something very *sweet*." He said it in a menacing way, with a mischievous grin and an evil-villain kind of laugh. I almost felt sorry for the girls.

"Let's go," Will said. He had the squirt gun ready in his hand. We headed upstairs and leaned over the railing above Hairy Wonder.

"Why are we stopping here?" I asked.

Patrick dropped his backpack and stared down at Hairy Wonder. "I overheard Tammy at Burger World. She said they were going to Hairy Wonder today. All we have to do is wait for them to show up."

So we waited and waited. I saw people with green hair and purple hair. One guy walked by with tattoos all over his body. One girl with long blond hair had six nose rings. A lot of people looked at the hair clips and headbands in the store window, but none of them was Tammy, Karen, or Angela. "Let's go home," I said. "This is stupid."

"Shhh," Will hissed and pointed. "There they are."

The three girls paused in front of the big window display at Hairy Wonder. As soon as they stopped, Will and Patrick went into action. Before I could say a word, Will ripped open my pillow and Patrick unscrewed a big jar of honey.

"Bombs away!" Patrick yelled. He dumped the honey out of the container right onto the girls' heads. Will was beside him, dumping the feathers. The feathers floated down like fluffy darts. Angela's pigtails were covered with feathers. Karen's curls dripped with honey, but Tammy's long blond hair had changed color completely. Tammy was a total featherhead. The girls looked like a henhouse had exploded on their heads.

Will laughed. "That'll teach them to throw eggs at us. Now they're the chickens!" Will and Patrick laughed before taking off running.

I was in shock. I'd heard of people being tarred and feathered in the colonial days, but I'd never heard of anyone being honeyed and feathered in the mall.

"Ahhhh!" the girls screamed and looked up. Patrick and Will were already gone. I was the only one left looking down at the three of them. But not for long. It only took me a second to race after Patrick and Will.

"We're going to get you for this, Justin!" Angela screamed.

"You'll be sorry," Tammy hollered. All I could hear from Karen was something that sounded like sobs. I felt like a first-class jerk, but I kept running.

Patrick and Will were already on their bikes, so I hopped on mine and sped off. Patrick and Will congratulated themselves the whole way home, but I didn't say anything. "See you tomorrow," Will yelled as he and Patrick rode by my house. I just grunted and pushed my bike into the garage.

When I got inside it was dinnertime and things didn't get any better. Dinner was my

13

mom's worst dish, tuna surprise. Some people might like tuna casserole, but those people don't have my mom cooking for them. Don't get me wrong, Mom can cook some great dinners, but her tuna casserole tastes like sewer sludge and nuclear waste mixed together — not that I've ever actually tasted nuclear waste or sewer sludge.

"What's wrong?" Mom asked after I barely touched my dinner.

I shrugged. "I guess I don't feel very well."

My mother put her hand on my forehead. "You don't feel hot," she said. "Would a surprise make you feel better?"

"Surprise?" I asked. I didn't think I could stand another tuna surprise tonight. I hoped Mom hadn't whipped up any experimental dessert. She liked to make up her own recipes. She tried weird stuff like spinach brownies and bubble-gum cake.

"This," Mom said, holding up a yellow envelope, "came for you by special delivery."

"No way!" I yelled as I grabbed the envelope and tore it open. "That's it!"

Chapter 3
DREAM COME TRUE

My hands were shaking so much, I could hardly get the letter out of the envelope. Finally, I leaned against the kitchen counter and read it to myself.

Dear Justin,

Congratulations! You have been chosen! You are invited to compete in The Slime Wars — the fantastic TV game show just for kids. Your adventure begins on July 10.

Good luck! Fabulous prizes like new bicycles and cash await your team — if you win — but the slime pit awaits the unlucky losers. Official rules are enclosed. Best wishes in your quest for the ultimate Slime Wars.

Sincerely,
Bob Burtstrum, The Slime Wars *Host*

I jumped around and around in circles. "All right!" I screamed, "I'm going to be rich!"

My mom looked at me like I had lost my mind. "What are you talking about?"

"I'm going to be on *The Slime Wars*," I told her.

"What's that?" she asked. "Does it hurt?"

I couldn't believe my own mom didn't even know about the coolest game show on TV. Had she just crawled out from under a rock? "It's a game show," I told her. "Your whole team can win brand-new bikes and a mountain of money."

"What do you have to do to win?" Mom asked.

"My team has to answer more questions than the other team," I told her. "Patrick,

Will, and I are going to have to study hard. If you lose, you have to go down a fifteen-foot slime slide. There's a pool of green goop at the bottom that you splat into."

Mom smiled and took the letter out of my hands. "I've been trying to get you to study forever. I should have threatened you with slime years ago.

"Uh-oh," Mom said. I got a little nervous. Mom never said *uh-oh* without a good reason.

Chapter 4
PLEASE

"You have to have three girls on your team," Mom said.

"No," I explained. "Each team has three people, boys or girls. That's the way they always play it."

Mom pointed to the bottom of the paper where there was small fine print. "It says to qualify for the *new* edition of *The Slime Wars* you must have three girls and three boys. It looks like they changed the rules."

"What?" I yelled. "How could they do that?"

Mom shrugged. "Maybe you could get the girls across the street to be on your team," she suggested.

"Why don't you just ground me for life instead?" I said.

"Don't be silly," Mom answered. "I'm sure the girls would like to win bicycles and money."

I knew the girls would like to win bicycles, but not with us. The chances of the girls agreeing to be on our team were as likely as aliens landing in my front yard. It was not going to happen.

"No way," Will said the next day. "We can't ask them for help. And besides, I don't want to play with them." We were in Patrick's backyard, up in his tree house. I had just told them about the letter.

"I'd really like a new bike," Patrick said. "Maybe the girls would, too."

"First, we have to ask them," I said.

Will held up his hand. "I'm not going to ask them."

"Oh, yes you are," I told him. "We all are. And we're going to apologize to them."

"Apologize!" Will shouted. "Are you crazy? They started it."

I folded my arms and stared at Will. Patrick frowned. Will rolled his eyes. The next thing I knew, we were crossing the street to Tammy and Karen's house.

Apologizing wasn't as easy as I thought it would be. The minute we stepped into their yard, we got hit with a tidal wave of water.

Karen's hose, water balloons from Tammy, and Angela's super squirt gun all hit us at the same time, from three different directions.

"Stop!" I screamed. "We want to apologize." The girls couldn't hear anything over the roar of their laughter, and I got a mouth full of water. There was nothing to do but run, and that's just what we did.

Will was spitting mad by the time we got to my yard. "That's it," he yelled. "There's no way I'm going to apologize to those dumb girls."

"But we need them if we want to get on the show," I told him. "There aren't any other girls our age on this entire block."

"Listen," Patrick said to me as he squeezed water out of his T-shirt. "I want a new bike and I want it bad. But nothing is

worth the humiliation of begging those girls to help us."

I sighed and looked across the street. The girls were still rolling on the ground, laughing at us.

"We can call some other girls from school," Patrick suggested as we went inside my house.

I shuddered. The idea of actually calling a girl was creepy, but it had to be done. We got out the school phone book and did the deed. Twenty phone calls later, we were out of luck.

"What's wrong with girls?" Will complained. "Why do they have to go on vacation? Why do they have to go to camp? Why do they have to visit their grandmothers?"

"It *is* summer," I reminded him. I sighed and looked out the window. The girls were still sitting in Tammy and Karen's yard with their hose, balloons, and squirt gun. There had to be some way for us to get the girls to join our team. But whatever it was, it wasn't going to be easy.

Chapter 5
SWEETS FOR THE
DRAGONS

I thought about it all evening until my head hurt. By the next morning, I finally had the answer. When my mom is mad at my dad, he buys her a present. Usually, that gets them kissing and making up. Of course, the thought of kissing Tammy, Karen, or Angela made me want to puke, but the present part might work. All I wanted was for them to agree to be on *The Slime Wars* with us.

I called Patrick and Will. "We need to talk," I said over the phone. "Let's meet at the mall."

By ten o'clock, we all stood in front of Arcade Castle. I told them my plan. Will yelled,

"No way! I'm not wasting my money on those dragon girls!"

"Listen," I said. "It won't cost that much. We can pick flowers from our backyards. All we need to do is buy them some candy."

"Let's make the candy," Patrick suggested. "And we could put some hot sauce in it for extra flavor."

Will laughed. "Maybe we could put some insect spray in there, too. That would make them *bug* off." Patrick slapped Will on the back and they both laughed.

"I'm serious," I said. "Ever since *The Slime Wars* came on TV, I've wanted to be on it. This is my one chance. I wanted to win and I thought my friends would help me. But all you guys want to do is goof off. Thanks for nothing." I started walking away.

"Oh, don't get all nuts on us," Patrick said. "We'll help. We were just kidding around."

Will nodded. "Come over to my house and we'll bake some brownies. I happen to know that Angela loves chocolate."

"Really?" I said.

"We had a class party last year, and she gulped down at least ten brownies," Will said.

I grinned. Maybe everything would work out after all. "You guys are the best," I said.

"We know," Patrick said. "I can't stand those girls, but I'm not going to let them stop me from winning a new bike."

"Or a pocketful of cold hard cash," Will said with a big smile on his face.

We raced over to Will's house and attacked his kitchen like a bunch of madmen. His mother almost had a heart attack when we told her what we wanted to do. But she let us use the kitchen as long as we promised to clean up the mess. She even showed us a good recipe and turned on the oven.

We poured, stirred, cracked, and stirred some more. "Not bad," I said, looking in the bowl.

"These are going to be the best brownies in the history of the world," Patrick said, licking a spoon.

"You're not supposed to do that," I informed him as I poured the batter into a pan. "You shouldn't eat anything that has raw eggs in it. You can get some disease."

Patrick grabbed his throat when I slid the pan into the oven. He fell on the floor as I closed the oven door.

"I'm dying," Patrick croaked, reaching for Will. "I have some horrible disease. Help me."

"My mom will kill us for real if we don't stop fooling around and start cleaning up," Will said. Will's kitchen was a disaster. How could one pan of brownies make such a mess? Sugar crunched under our sneakers and chocolate powder covered every available counter space.

I grabbed a sponge, Will started sweeping, and Patrick put bowls in the dishwasher. Before long, a delicious chocolaty smell came from the oven.

"Maybe we could eat a couple of these ourselves before we take them over to the girls," I suggested. "To make sure they taste okay."

"Sounds good to me," Patrick said, "but what about the flowers?"

"Mom has some pink roses out in the backyard," Will suggested. "We could cut a few of those." We headed into Will's back-yard and came back with a handful of pretty roses. When we got inside, the brownies didn't smell good anymore. They smelled burned. In fact, smoke was pouring out of the oven.

"Fire!" Will screamed.

Chapter 6
BURNED

Okay, it wasn't a fire. But the brownies were pretty burned around the edges. "They're ruined," I said.

"They look like dried dinosaur poop, if you ask me," Patrick said.

I was beginning to feel like dinosaur doo-doo myself. Winning a bike seemed impossible.

"These brownies aren't so bad," Will told us. "My dad burns stuff like this all the time." He took a butter knife, chopped away the crunchy edges, and put the rest on a plate. I had to admit they didn't look half bad.

"We'd better test them," Patrick suggested. He took a big bite and talked while he chewed. "These are awesome."

"Let me try," Will said. By the time we'd

all eaten a couple, the plate full of brownies looked a little skimpy.

"The girls are going to know we ate most of them," I said.

"No, they won't," Will said. He got out a smaller plate and piled the brownies on it. "Presto, a full plate of brownies."

"We'd better take them to the girls before they're all gone," I suggested.

Will groaned. "Why don't you go by yourself?" Will asked. "You can tell the girls we're sorry."

I shook my head. "We're all in this together." I grabbed the plate of brownies and shoved the flowers into Will's hands.

"They're probably going to cut off our hair with a Weed Whacker and drop us in boiling hair spray," Patrick complained.

"They are not," I said. "Now, let's get going." I headed toward the street, gripping the plate of brownies like it was a life preserver. Actually, it sort of was. I hoped the brownies and the flowers would be enough to save us from being dropped in boiling hair spray.

I looked both ways and stepped into the street. Will grabbed my arm and pulled me back onto the sidewalk. "What's wrong?" I asked. "There aren't any cars coming."

"I just had an idea," Will explained. He pushed the roses into Patrick's hands and raced back into his house. Three minutes later he came out with a white washcloth tied onto an empty paper towel roll.

Will smiled and waved the washcloth. "I surrender," he said.

"Good idea," Patrick said. "Now, maybe the girls will listen to us *before* they massacre us."

"They're not going to massacre us," I told Patrick as we crossed over the center line to the north side of the street. "They're girls, not commandos."

Will raised his flag like a sword. "We're about to find out, because here they come." We walked down the sidewalk toward the girls' houses and they walked toward us.

They didn't come empty-handed. Each girl held a big, fat juicy tomato in each hand.

I knew what they were planning to do, so I talked fast. "We come in peace," I said.

Will waved his white washcloth flag. "We want to call a truce."

The girls raised their tomatoes like they were getting ready to take aim. Patrick blurted out, "We want to help you win brand-new bicycles."

Tammy lifted one eyebrow. "What are you talking about?" she asked.

I held the plate of brownies out as a peace offering and Patrick held out the roses.

"What are you guys trying to do?" Karen asked. "Poison us?"

Patrick grabbed a brownie off the plate and stuffed it into his mouth. "They're good."

Angela licked her lips, but kept the tomatoes in her hands. I could tell she wanted a brownie bad. Maybe this would work.

"Here's the deal," I explained. "Patrick, Will, and I have been asked to be on *The Slime Wars*. The first prizes are new bikes and lots of money."

"I don't believe you," Karen said. "That's

a great game show. They wouldn't ask you jerks to be on it."

"It's true," Will snapped. "Justin has the letter to prove it." I didn't say a word. I just pulled the letter out of my shorts pocket and held it up.

The girls didn't say anything, but I could tell they were impressed. "What's that got to do with us?" Tammy asked.

"They changed the rules," I explained. "We have to have a team of three boys *and* three girls."

"Will you do it with us?" Patrick asked.

The three girls looked at one another. Then they held their tomatoes up. I had an awful feeling their answer was going to be a definite NO.

Chapter 7
BAMBOOZLED

The next thing I knew, we were sitting in Tammy and Karen's kitchen. The girls were pigging out on our brownies, the roses were in a big green vase, and we were being bamboozled.

My dad says being bamboozled means being tricked. It seemed to me the girls were definitely taking advantage of us.

"We'll do it," Tammy said, "under the following conditions."

Will, Patrick, and I held our breath. There was no telling what the girls would ask for.

"First of all," Tammy said, wiping brownie crumbs off her cheek, "we get half of all the money won."

Will, Patrick, and I nodded our heads. That seemed fair enough. But the girls weren't happy with fair. Next, they got greedy.

Karen smiled. "Secondly," she said, like a lawyer on TV, "you must agree to be nice to us."

Angela giggled. "You have to carry our books to school for a whole month."

Will jumped up from the table. "There's no way!" he shouted. I grabbed his arm and made him sit down.

"It's not that bad," I told Will. "We could do that. We'll have our new bikes to ride on . . . our shiny new bikes." After all, Angela hadn't said anything about us walking or riding *with* them.

Will nodded. "Oh, all right."

I looked at Patrick. He just rolled his eyes and sighed. "I guess it won't kill me," he said in a sad-sounding voice.

"Then it's agreed," Tammy said.

Karen held up a brownie like a bomb. "There's just one more thing," she said. "You have to do our chores for a whole month."

This time Patrick jumped up from the

table. Patrick hated to do his own chores, so he certainly wouldn't want to do anyone else's. "All the money in the world couldn't make me do your chores!" Patrick snapped.

The girls could tell they had gone too far. "All right," Tammy said. "We're willing to negotiate. We'll change it to just one little week."

The girls folded their arms over their chests and stared at us. Patrick and Will folded their arms over their chests and stared back. I could tell that things were going downhill fast. So, being a noble kind of guy, I did a noble thing. (Actually, I was a desperate guy doing a desperate thing, but noble sounds so much better.)

"*I* will do all your chores for a week," I told the girls. "If you agree to be on the game show with us. And if you agree to no more conditions."

The girls were in shock. I was a bit in shock myself. Had I gone crazy?

The girls nodded. "All right," Tammy said.

"It's agreed. We'll draw up a contract and you can sign it. Then it will be official."

I gulped. It was really going to happen. I was going to be on *The Slime Wars*. My head felt a little funny.

"Wait a minute," Karen said. "There's one more thing we have to discuss."

Chapter 8
PRACTICE LIKE CRAZY

"We have to set up a practice schedule," Karen told us.

"What for?" Will asked.

"So we can win the game, of course," Tammy said.

Angela nodded and ate the last brownie. She talked with her mouth half full. "If we're going to do this, we're going to have to study like crazy. How long before the show?"

"It's July tenth," I told her.

Karen's eyes got big. "That means we only have two weeks to study. Thank goodness it's summer. We can work from sunup to sundown."

Will shook his head. "Wait just a minute," he said. "There's no way I'm spending my summer studying. It's bad enough we have to study the rest of the year at school."

"Don't you want to win the bicycles and the money?" Tammy asked.

"Yeah, but not if it's going to kill me," Will said matter-of-factly.

"A little studying never killed anybody," Karen said, pushing her blond hair out of her eyes. "It might even do you some good."

Patrick groaned, and I stood up to leave. "Well, we'd better get going," I said. "The guys and I will study at my house starting tomorrow."

Tammy shook her head. "No way! If we're going to win *The Slime Wars* together, we're going to have to study together."

Two weeks of studying with the terrible trio of Daleside Drive didn't sound like a good idea. We might actually knock one another's brains out before the contest started. I tried to talk the girls out of it. Will tried to talk the girls out of it. Patrick tried to talk the girls out of it. Nothing worked.

Tammy looked at her watch. "Let's meet here tomorrow morning exactly at eight. We'll start with history."

"History is boring," Will told Tammy.

"You think wars and sword fighting are boring?" Tammy asked.

"No, sword fights are cool," Will said, "but what does that have to do with history?"

"Most of history is about fighting, silly," Karen told Patrick.

"All right," I said. "So we'll study history first and then we'll study science."

"Boring," Angela said. "Why can't we learn about something fun, like movies and movie stars?"

"Because it's *The Slime Wars,* not the Moron Dumbo game," Will said.

"Are you calling me dumb?" Angela held up a fist to Will.

Will pretended to be scared by falling to his knees. "Oh, no," he teased. "She's going to hurt me. Call 911."

Angela grabbed the vase of roses and

pulled the roses out. She dumped the green water right on Will's head.

"Arrrgh," Will yelled and threw the brownie crumbs at Angela. I grabbed Will, and Tammy grabbed Angela.

"Come on," I told Will. Luckily Will and Patrick came outside without a fight. We stopped in Tammy's yard. Will's hair still had little green leaves in it from the roses. He definitely looked mad.

I hoped the girls would behave themselves tomorrow, because Will looked ready to fight. And a fight would mean the end of *The Slime Wars* for all of us.

Chapter 9
PERFECT GENTLEMEN

"How can you stand them?" I asked Will and Patrick. We had studied for four days at Tammy's house and I was about to go insane. The girls were always giggling about some stupid fact or flinging their hair back out of their faces. Why didn't they just cut their hair off if they always had to push it back? It was enough to drive a guy crazy. But somehow, Will and Patrick just smiled and skimmed through encyclopedia after encyclopedia looking for important information. They never complained, never even said an angry word. They were perfect gentlemen.

"Those girls are driving me crazy," I told Will and Patrick as we left Tammy's house. Will looked back to make sure none of the girls was watching. Then he pulled pink plugs out of each ear. "You should try these," he said with a smile.

Patrick laughed. "Those are good, but mini headphones are much better." He pulled up his shirt to expose a small CD player with wires running up his stomach. He turned around to show me the wires behind his ears.

"I've been suffering for four days," I complained. "Why didn't you tell me earlier?"

"This whole thing was your idea," Will said. "We figured you wanted to enjoy the full experience."

Just then Tammy stuck her head out the door. Patrick quickly pulled his shirt down. "Boys!" Tammy screamed, like we were two miles away instead of right in front of her house.

"What?" Patrick hollered back.

"You don't have to yell," Tammy said. "I just wanted to tell you we're planning to meet at Coldstream's Department Store after dinner tonight."

"What for?" Will asked.

Tammy rolled her eyes. "We have to pick out matching outfits, of course." She shut the door before Will could say another word.

The three of us broke out laughing. "Matching outfits?" Patrick squealed. "Right! Like we're really going to wear matching outfits. What do those girls think we are? Total nerds?"

A week and a half later we were sitting in the waiting room for *The Slime Wars* wearing — you guessed it — matching outfits. The girls had picked out blue shorts and white shirts with a blue design on the pocket. For matching clothes, they weren't too bad — a little nerdy, but not *too* bad. Will didn't agree.

"I can't believe we're going to be on television looking like something left over from when my mom went to school," Will complained.

Tammy tossed her blond hair back out of her face. "You happen to look very nice. Besides, it's a proven fact that when you look good you perform better."

Angela gulped. "In that case, I hope we look really good. I'm so nervous I think I could throw up."

"Don't stand next to me," Will said. Then, as if he felt sorry for Angela, he said, "Don't worry. You'll do great."

Angela smiled at Will. "I'm sure you'll do fine, too."

"All this sweet talk is making me sick," Patrick said. "How much longer are we going to have to wait?"

"It seems like we've been here for hours," Karen agreed.

Tammy checked her watch. "No, we've only been waiting for twenty minutes."

Just then the door marked STAGE opened and a woman in a pink suit smiled at us. "It's time," she said. "Please follow me."

The girls all squealed. I just looked at Will and Patrick. Their faces looked paler than their new shirts. "This is it," I said with a gulp.

Chapter 10
THE SHOW

"This is so cool," Will whispered as we entered the set. Neon lights flashed everywhere and cameras pointed at us. For a few minutes, I couldn't see a thing.

"Let's all say hello to the Daleside Dream Team," the announcer, Bob Burtstrum, said into the microphone as my eyes adjusted. Will, Patrick, and I cringed at the stupid name the girls had made up.

Bob and the entire studio audience of about fifty people said, "HELLLLLLL-OOOOO, Daleside Dream Team!" to us. I knew my mom was in the audience somewhere, but the lights were so bright I couldn't see her.

All six of us ran over to our seats just like

I'd seen other kids do when I'd watched the show. We stood behind an orange desk with a huge sign that read: DALESIDE DREAM TEAM. Each of us had a big green buzzer to push when we knew an answer. Bob Burtstrum stood on a high platform between us and the other team. Bob had on a dark green tuxedo that made him look like a big lizard. The other team looked older than us, and they were dressed in matching striped shirts. They looked smart. I hoped we looked smart, too.

Under Bob's platform was the green slime pit. That's where the losers landed after dropping down a fifteen-foot slime slide. I gulped and hoped I wouldn't see any slime close up today.

"Now that we've met our players," Bob Burtstrum announced, "let's start the fun."

The audience cheered and I grinned. This was it. I was really on *The Slime Wars*. I felt a little woozy. Karen must have felt funny, too, because I saw Patrick patting her on the hand.

"And the categories are: Math, History, Famous People, and Science," Bob announced. "Our first question is from the History category."

Everyone held their hands over their buzzers as Bob asked the question, "What battle is considered the bloodiest —"

Will slammed his hand on the buzzer. "Oops," he said. My eyes rolled back in my head. Will had hit the buzzer too soon! Now, he had to answer without hearing the rest of the question.

Everyone's eyes turned to Will. Will bit his lip. I knew Will liked sword fighting and battles; maybe he knew the answer. I looked at the slime pit. Maybe he didn't know the answer, and we were doomed. I cringed.

"The answer is . . . the Battle of Antietam from the Civil War," Will said in a shaky voice.

Bob Burtstrum looked at Will. "You are absolutely . . . correct."

"Yes!" my team shouted. Angela gave Will

a big hug and I gave him a big slap on the back.

It was fantastic. We were one point up and Bob hadn't even asked one full question yet. I looked at the other team and smiled. They didn't look so smart anymore.

Bob asked his next question. "What is the name of the theorem —"

A tall boy on the other team hit his buzzer. "The Pythagorean theorem," the boy said loudly.

"You are exactly right," Bob said with a smile. Then to the audience, Bob said, "These kids are so smart, I may not get to talk much today."

The audience laughed, but I was worried. The other team looked smarter already. The slime pit bubbled and my head started to ache.

"For our next question, we turn to our Famous People category," Bob said. Everyone had their hands ready.

Bob smiled at us with big white teeth. "What cartoon character lives in —"

The other team hit the buzzer. I wanted to sink down behind the orange desk. I wanted to go anywhere but the slime pit.

Chapter 11
DOWNHILL FAST

The tall kid from the other team said, "The answer is Jimmy Neutron. He lives in space."

Bob looked at his answer card and shook his head. "I'm sorry," he said, "that is incorrect." I wanted to jump up and kiss Bob on the cheek, I was so happy. I settled for a hug from Tammy.

At first, I wanted to puke when Tammy grabbed me, but then it wasn't so bad. I didn't have much time to think about it because Bob started talking again.

"Finally, I get to finish my first question of the day." Bob flashed a big smile at the audience and they laughed. He turned toward our team.

"What cartoon character," Bob said again, "lives in a pineapple under the sea?"

I looked at Will and shrugged. The other team glanced at one another. Nobody knew the answer. I wondered if both teams would end up in the slime pit if we tied. It looked like we were about to find out, but then Angela hit her buzzer just before time ran out.

Everyone looked at Angela. I couldn't believe she had actually hit the buzzer. Angela was not exactly an intellectual. She was more into movies and going to the mall than actually thinking. "The answer is SpongeBob SquarePants," Angela said quickly.

Our team held their breath. All eyes turned to Bob. He smiled and said, "You are absolutely . . . correct!"

This time I would have hugged anyone and I did. Everyone on our team was so happy, we were hugging one another like old married people. The crowd cheered. Let me tell you, it was fantastic. Too bad it didn't last. After that, things started going downhill fast. The other team got the question about science. In fact, they got the next two questions.

Then Bob announced it was time for a commercial break.

The lady in the pink suit led us back to the waiting room. Tammy's face was so red I thought she might explode. "I am *not* — I repeat — *not* going to go down that slime slide," Tammy said.

I shrugged my shoulders. "Things might look pretty bad right now," I said, "but it's not over yet."

Tammy pointed her finger at me. "This was all your nutty idea!"

"If we go down the slide, it'll be your fault!" Karen said angrily. "We'll never forgive you!"

Will stood beside me. "Hey, we all wanted to be on the show," he said. "And we all took the slime risk."

Tammy folded her arms in front of her chest. "This isn't fair. I never thought we would lose. I've never lost at anything important."

"We haven't lost yet," Patrick told her.

Angela nodded her head. "We can't give up. We could still make a comeback."

Tammy didn't look too hopeful. I didn't feel we had a chance, but I put on a brave front. I felt like the coach of a losing football team. "We've got to get back in there," I told them, "and show that other team what the kids from Daleside Drive are made of."

"That's right," Patrick said, slapping me on the back. "We'll beat the pants off those geeks and we'll laugh when they're sliding around in the slime."

"Do you really think so?" Karen asked Patrick.

Patrick nodded. "Of course," he said bravely.

Karen smiled at Patrick, which was a lot better than the look Tammy gave me. Tammy definitely looked like she would kill me if we got dumped into the slime pit.

Chapter 12
SLIME CITY

We came back big. We answered enough questions to tie the other team. Unfortunately, the next question was the last.

"Our last category," Bob announced, "is our tie-breaker. And the category is Famous People."

Our whole team looked at Angela. She smiled and shrugged her shoulders. It made me nervous to think the outcome of my whole *Slime Wars* career depended on how many movie magazines Angela had read lately.

I guess Bob didn't think we were nervous enough because he said, "This question is our final question. It's the whole ball of wax . . . the big one . . . the whole enchilada."

I wanted to scream at Bob to just get on with it. Tammy looked like she could scream, too. She didn't. She just glared at me and whispered, "If I land in that slime pit, I'm going to get you." I could tell she meant it, too.

I gulped as Bob read the question. "What famous person directed a —"

Buzz! All of our eyes turned to Patrick. I could feel the ooze getting closer. I knew that Patrick knew nothing about famous people, let alone directors. We were in big trouble.

Patrick cleared his throat and squeaked, "George Lucas." Yes! I had forgotten about the *Star Wars* movies. Patrick loved them. Of course he would know that George Lucas directed them.

What a great team I had put together. Patrick had really come through for us. I could hardly wait to ride my new bike. I could hardly wait to spend my big wad of money. I'd never have to worry about my allowance again.

Bob Burtstrum snapped me out of my

daydream. He was talking again. "I'm sorry," he told Patrick. "That is incorrect."

Incorrect! Incorrect? My head started spinning as Bob finished the question. "What famous person directed the movie *E.T.*, then later went on to make cartoons?"

Tammy slammed on her buzzer. Too late! It was the other team's chance to answer. The leader of the other team smiled at me before saying in a smug voice, "Steven Spielberg."

Bob's next words will forever ring in my ears. "Correct! You are the winners!"

The next sixty seconds were the most horrible in my entire life. Bells rang. Lights flashed and the floor underneath my team's feet opened. We slid down a long slide. I could hear Tammy's screams just before we hit the big pool of green slime.

Splash! We were in the pit. Will's face was covered with slime. Our white shirts were covered with green ooze.

Actually, it was kind of cool. Patrick splashed everyone, and I felt like a swamp

monster. I laughed when I saw Angela's pigtails dripping green slime. We started tossing slime at one another. Even though we lost, everyone was having a good time. Well, almost everyone.

I stopped laughing when I saw Tammy. She was glaring at me and she was mad. At that exact moment, I knew that the war between the boys and girls of Daleside Drive was just beginning.

ABOUT THE AUTHORS

Debbie Dadey is the author and coauthor of more than one hundred children's books, including *The Adventures of the Bailey School Kids* books and *Ghostville Elementary*. Debbie lives in Fort Collins, Colorado, with her family and two dogs. Nathan Dadey is Debbie's teenage son and this is his first book. *The Slime Wars* was a summer project that got a little slimy.

Ready for some spooky fun?

Ghostville Elementary

from best-selling authors,
Marcia Thornton Jones and Debbie Dadey!

The basement of Sleepy Hollow's elementary school is haunted. At least that's what everyone says. But no one has ever gone downstairs to prove it. Until now . . .

This year, Cassidy and Jeff's classroom is in the basement. But the kids aren't scared. There's no such thing as ghosts, right?

Tell that to the ghosts.

The basement belongs to another class — a *ghost* class. They don't want to share. And they will haunt Cassidy and her friends until they get their room back!

Creepy, weird, wacky, and
funny things happen to
the Bailey School Kids!™
Collect and read them all!

The Adventures of

THE
BAILEY SCHOOL
KIDS®

The Adventures of THE BAILEY SCHOOL KIDS®

❏ BSK 0-439-04398-0	#38 Ninjas Don't Bake Pumpkin Pie	$3.99 US
❏ BSK 0-439-04399-9	#39 Dracula Doesn't Rock and Roll	$3.99 US
❏ BSK 0-439-04401-4	#40 Sea Monsters Don't Ride Motorcycles	$3.99 US
❏ BSK 0-439-04400-6	#41 The Bride of Frankenstein Doesn't Bake Cookies	$3.99 US
❏ BSK 0-439-21582-X	#42 Robots Don't Catch Chicken Pox	$3.99 US
❏ BSK 0-439-21583-8	#43 Vikings Don't Wear Wrestling Belts	$3.99 US
❏ BSK 0-439-21584-6	#44 Ghosts Don't Rope Wild Horses	$3.99 US
❏ BSK 0-439-36803-0	#45 Wizards Don't Wear Graduation Gowns	$3.99 US
❏ BSK 0-439-36805-7	#46 Sea Serpents Don't Juggle Water Balloons	$3.99 US

❏ BSK 0-439-04396-4	Bailey School Kids Super Special #4: Mrs. Jeepers in Outer Space	$3.99 US
❏ BSK 0-439-21585-4	Bailey School Kids Super Special #5: Mrs. Jeepers' Monster Class Trip	$3.99 US
❏ BSK 0-439-30641-8	Bailey School Kids Super Special #6: Mrs. Jeepers On Vampire Island	$3.99 US
❏ BSK 0-439-40831-8	Bailey School Kids Holiday Special: Aliens Don't Carve Jack-o'-lanterns	$3.99 US
❏ BSK 0-439-40832-6	Bailey School Kids Holiday Special: Mrs. Claus Doesn't Climb Telephone Poles	$3.99 US
❏ BSK 0-439-33338-5	Bailey School Kids Thanksgiving Special: Swampmonsters Don't Chase Wild Turkeys	$3.99 US

Available wherever you buy books, or use this order form

Scholastic Inc., P.O. Box 7502, Jefferson City, MO 65102

Please send me the books I have checked above. I am enclosing $_____ (please add $2.00 to cover shipping and handling). Send check or money order — no cash or C.O.D.s please.

Name _____

Address _____

City _____ State/Zip _____

Please allow four to six weeks for delivery. Offer good in the U.S. only. Sorry, mail orders are not available to residents of Canada. Prices subject to change.

BSK902

Anything can happen when you wave your magic wand!

Abracadabra!

$3.99 each!